This book was made especially for:

❦ Mackenzie ❧

Dear Mackenzie,

How curious and brave you are! A wonderful journey awaits you in the pages of this book. Travel among some of the world's most fascinating countries and take it all in—but be sure to return home at the end! It would never be the same here without you.

With love:

Brave and intrepid, Mackenzie set out to explore the world piece by piece. What marvelous wonders were in her first stop: the land of the ancients called Greece!

 CAN YOU FIND MACKENZIE IN GREECE?

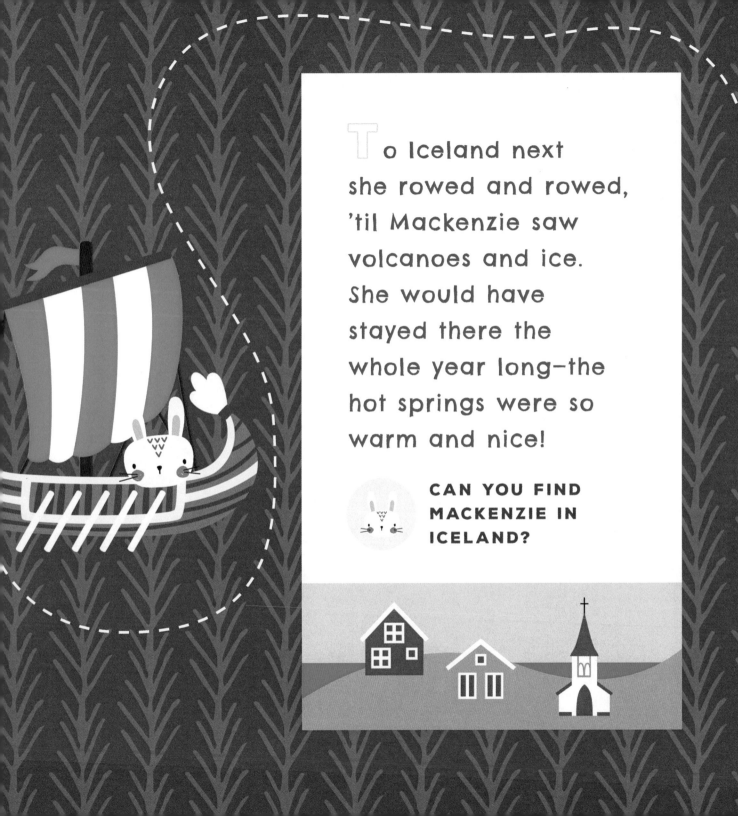

To Iceland next she rowed and rowed, 'til Mackenzie saw volcanoes and ice. She would have stayed there the whole year long—the hot springs were so warm and nice!

CAN YOU FIND MACKENZIE IN ICELAND?

But on she sailed to Germany next, an old-fashioned, storybook treat. There was gingerbread, bratwurst, streudel, and schnitzel— so many *great* things to eat!

CAN YOU FIND MACKENZIE IN GERMANY?

GERMANY

ROSTOCK

HAMBURG

Elbe

Oder

BREMEN

Ems

Berlin

Spree

HANNOVER

ESSEN

KÖLN

LEIPZIG

DREZDEN

Weser

FRANKFURT AM MAIN

Rhine

STUTTGART

Danube

MÜNCHEN

N
W E
S

To Brazil she went next just in time to explore the magic of Carnival! What lights, what costumes, what music there was! But with the tide, she soon left it all.

 CAN YOU FIND MACKENZIE IN BRAZIL?

MANAUS

OLA

BRAZILIA

BOLIVIA

RIO de JANEIRO

ARGENTINA

BRAZIL

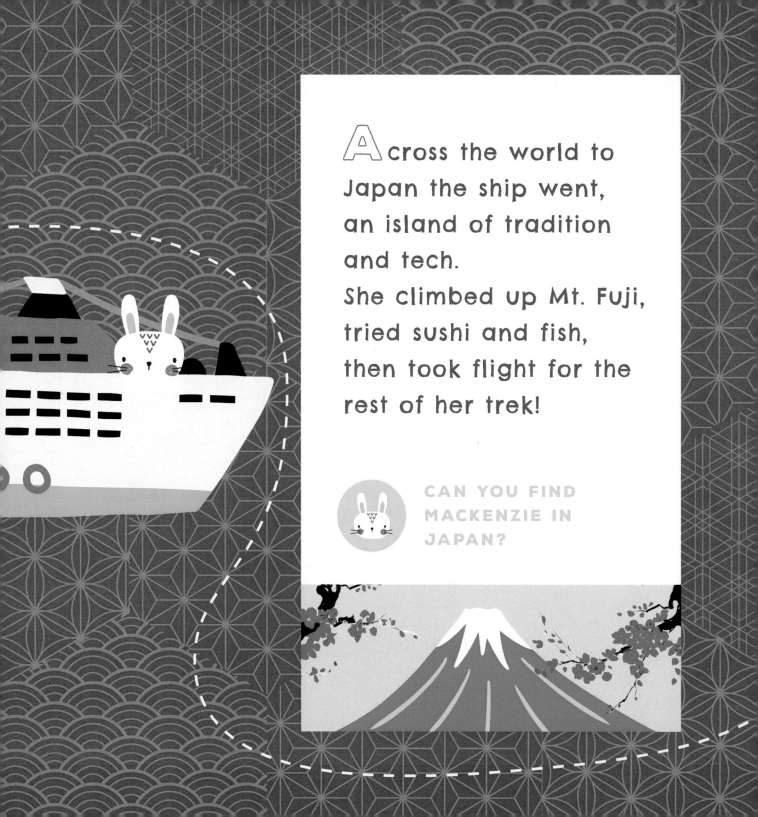

Across the world to Japan the ship went, an island of tradition and tech.
She climbed up Mt. Fuji, tried sushi and fish, then took flight for the rest of her trek!

CAN YOU FIND MACKENZIE IN JAPAN?

JAPAN

日本

SAPPORO

AOMORI

AKITA

SENDAI

NIIGATA

TOKYO

YOKOHAMA

NAGOYA

OSAKA

HIROSHIMA

FUKUOKA

KOCHI

NAGASAKI

MIYAZAKI

YAKUSHIMA

OKINAWA

ISHIGAKI

Off to the Netherlands she flew on her kite to see the tulips and dikes. She fished and tried waffles and watched the windmills, then sped off on her new Dutch bike!

CAN YOU FIND MACKENZIE IN THE NETHERLANDS?

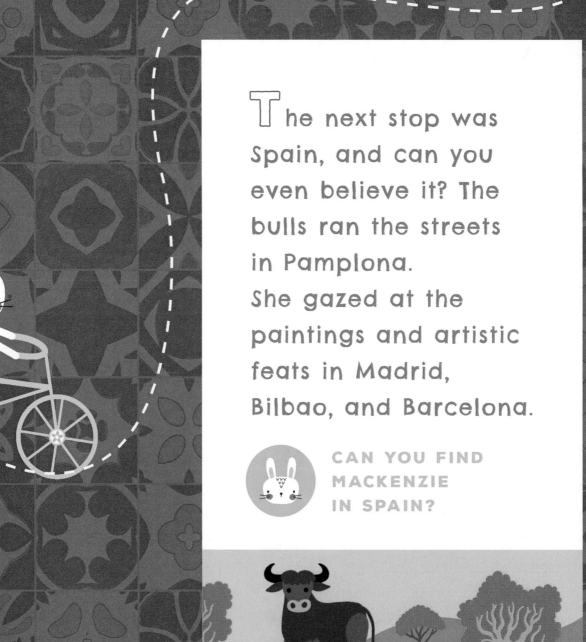

The next stop was Spain, and can you even believe it? The bulls ran the streets in Pamplona.
She gazed at the paintings and artistic feats in Madrid, Bilbao, and Barcelona.

CAN YOU FIND MACKENZIE IN SPAIN?

To the green isle of Ireland Mackenzie went next.
The castles were something to see!
She kissed an old stone and joined in a jig,
then set sail once again on the sea.

CAN YOU FIND MACKENZIE IN IRELAND?

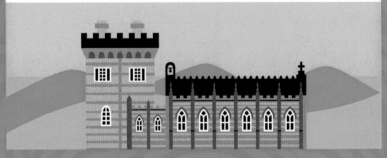

GALWAY

DUBLIN

KILKENNY

LIMERICK

WATERFORD

CORK

IRELAND

Shannon

Barrow

Suir

In Italy she landed
and to her surprise,
the country was
shaped like a boot!
In Rome, she did as
the Romans do,
and ate pasta,
gelato, and . . . fruit.

**CAN YOU FIND
MACKENZIE IN
ITALY?**

Italy

Hong Kong was next, and the buildings there shone with business and commerce and light. Mackenzie had dumplings and criss-crossed the ferry, then set sail again in the night.

 CAN YOU FIND MACKENZIE IN HONG KONG?

HONG KONG

KOWLOON

香留齒

單眼佬涼茶

TSIM
SHA
TSUI

CENTRAL

MID-LEVEL

I ♥ 香港

VAN CHAI

VICTORIA PEAK

HAPPY VALLEY

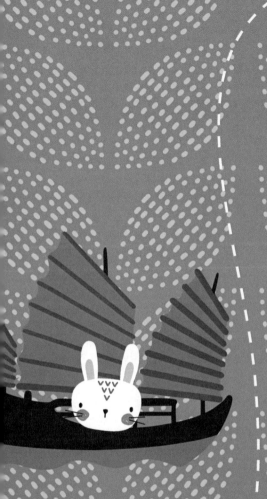

The ship arrived in Denmark at last, a place nearly surrounded by sea! She saw the Tin Soldier and brave Little Mermaid and had tea with the prince and the queen.

CAN YOU FIND MACKENZIE IN DENMARK?

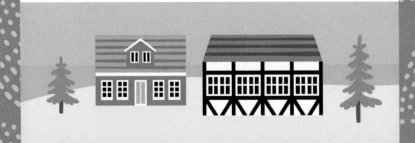

Then on, on to France, where the lavender grew and the tower called Eiffel stood tall. From Paris to Nice, Mackenzie saw every inch—she wanted to take in it all!

CAN YOU FIND MACKENZIE IN FRANCE?

FRANCE

LILLE

RENNES

NANTES

PARIS

STRASBOURG

BORDEAUX

LYON

MONTPELLIER

TOULOUSE

MARSEILLE

NICE

Across the Atlantic her little craft went to the shores of old Mexico.
She danced to the sounds of the mariachi band (with her ears tucked inside her sombrero).

CAN YOU FIND MACKENZIE IN MEXICO?

Back in her balloon, she sailed through the night until reaching the land of her own. She snuggled in bed and dreamed all night long of the wonderful earth she called home!

 IF YOU COULD TRAVEL ANYWHERE, WHERE WOULD *YOU* WANT TO VISIT?

Cover and book design by David Miles

Artwork created using elements from the following talented Shutterstock.com artists: Italy, Ireland, Spain, Netherlands, Greece, Iceland, Denmark, and Germany maps (Beskova Ekaterina); rabbit face (Sko Helen); hot air balloon (Iyeyee); around the world (R-i-s-e); falling stars (Nina_FOX); Mexico poster (Doni Hariyanto); Italy poster, France poster, Amsterdam poster, Germany poster (alaver); Denmark poster (Stanislav Novoselov); Hong Kong poster (Vector Tradition); Ireland poster (nastyrekh); Spain poster (Pavel Smolyakov); Japan poster (Ikanimo); Brazil poster (Anthony Krikoryan); Iceland poster (Red monkey); Greece poster (Anita_MI); bed, orange tree, houseplants, dresser, lamp (Ardea-studio); French pattern (traffico); Mexico elements (Katflare); Mexican pattern (Moon Meadows); Mexcio typography (Julio Aldana); Mexico map (helgascandinavus); Paris buildings, Golden Gate Bridge (Olga Zakharova); France map (lesyaskripak); Denmark pattern (PACPUMI); Hong Kong pattern (LauraKick); bamboo (VikiVector); Italian pattern (image4stock); fishing boat (Little Monster 2070); Irish pattern (Volodymyr Leus); Spanish pattern (Iva Villi); bunny on bicycle (svinka); Netherlands pattern (Ms Moloko); Japan pattern (marukopum); Japanese kites (Elsbet); cherry trees (Daiquiri); Japanese wave pattern (NokHoOkNoi); Japan typography (geen graphy); Japan and Hong Kong maps (Wondermilkycolor); Brazil pattern (EastFire); German pattern (dinadankersdesign); Iceland pattern (Yurta); Greece pattern (ALYOHAE); red bus (Gareth Cowlin); Eiffel tower and Notre-Dame (Anastasiia Kucherenko); Taipei locations (JoyImage); Brazil map (GoodStudio); miscellaneous world landmarks (Rimma Z).